THE FIRST THOUSAND WORDS

A Picture Word Book

Heather Amery
Illustrated by Stephen Cartwright

Consultant: Betty Root

At home

bathroom

living room

bath
soap
tap
bubbles
toothbrush
water
towel
sponge
shower
toothpaste
washbasin
toilet
bookcase
table
radio

4

radiator
wool
wallpaper
clock
carpet
cushion
record player

bedroom

hall

lamp

bed

chest

brush

pillow

wardrobe

rug

pictures

eiderdown

clothes

comb

mirror

sheet

stairs

spider

fly

pegs

cobweb

newspaper

chair

letters

telephone

The kitchen

refrigerator

glasses

clock

spoons

apron

switch

saucepans

saucers

iron

kettle

mop

vacuum cleaner

sink

forks

door

duster

stool

knives

polish

cooker

tiles

drawer

rubbish

frying pan

washing machine

dustpan

plates

ironing board

washing powder

brush

cupboard

table

bulb

cups

teaspoons

matches

key

broom

bowls

The garden

wheelbarrow

beehive

snail

bricks

dustbin

caterpillar

spade

ant

pigeon

gutter

ladder

seeds

8   shed

worm

flowers

sprinkler

bone

hedge

trowel

lawn mower

path

tree

fork

leaves

broom

hosepipe

hoe

smoke

bee

rake

pram

wasp

plants

grass

bonfire

bird's nest

sticks

greenhouse

9

The workshop

sandpaper

drill

bolts

tacks

saw

sawdust

hammer

file

tool box

screwdriver

plank

paint pot

shavings

penknife

10

barrel

axe

nuts

tape measure

screws

ladder

nails

vice

firewood

bench

jars

wood

plane

11

The street

garage

ambulance

bicycle

hole

café

pavement

shop

traffic lights

chimney

lorry

crossing

steps

man

12

hotel

police car

roller

drill

school

playground

flats

statue

bus

taxi

trailer

pipes

roof

market

factory

aerial

van

policeman

fire engine

house

lamp post

woman

digger

church

cinema

car

motor cycle

driver

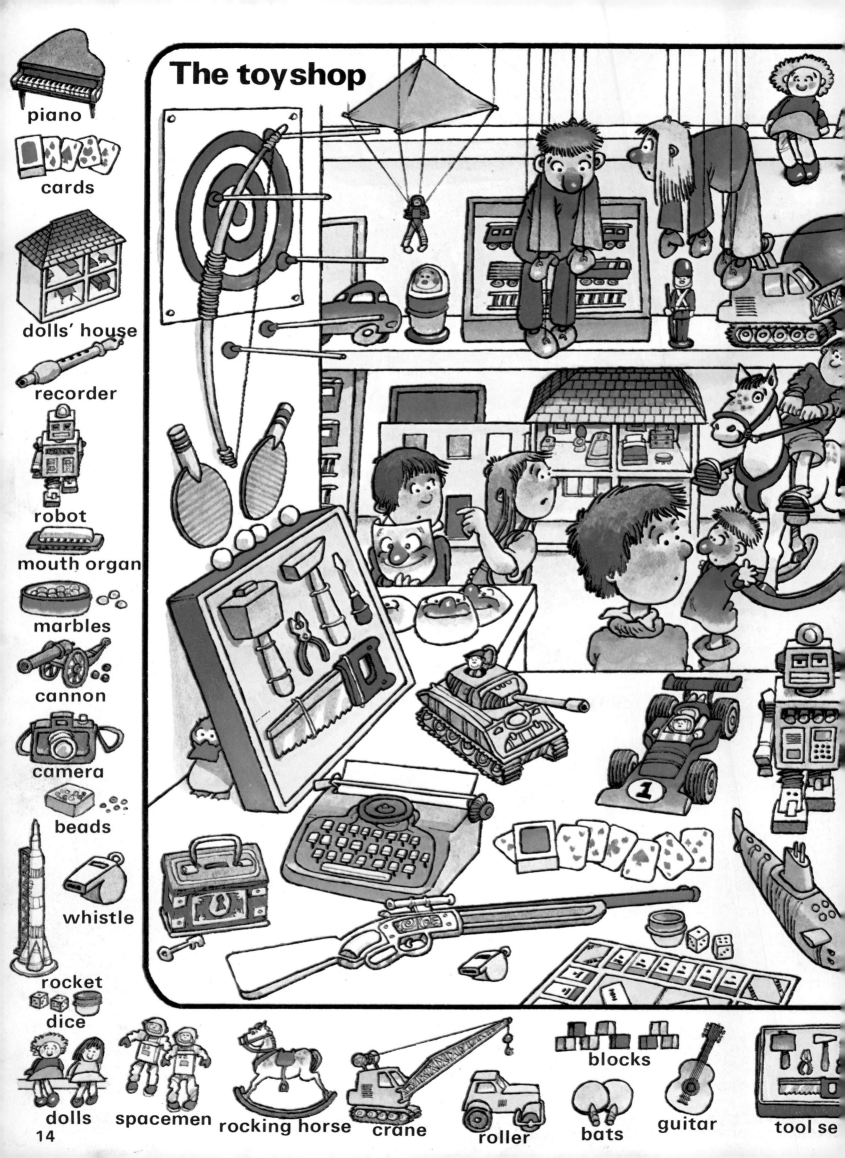

The toy shop

piano

cards

dolls' house

recorder

robot

mouth organ

marbles

cannon

camera

beads

whistle

rocket

dice

dolls

spacemen

rocking horse

crane

roller

bats

blocks

guitar

tool set

14

fishing rod

paints

clay

parachute

typewriter

boat

target

tank

soldiers

castle

money box

train set

drums

balls

puppets

racing car

masks

trumpet

bow and arrow

gun

submarine

15

The park

ball

string

sandpit

picnic

kite

ice cream

dog

swings

gate

path

tadpoles

slide

frog

bush

roller skates

children

scooter

16

swans

baby

earth

railings

push chair

birds

seesaw

flowers

puddle

ducklings

skipping rope

yacht

flower bed

bench

lake

dog lead

duck

trees 17

The zoo

panda

bat

penguin

hippopotamus

paws

kangaroo

wing

eagle

feathers

ostrich

giraffe

wolf

monkey

pelican

gorilla

bear

lion

beaver

cubs

crocodile

horns

deer

camel

seal

polar bear

apes

trunk

zebra

elephant

tail

buffalo

rhinoceros

shark

goat

dolphin

leopard

whale

tiger

19

The railway station

The garage

railway lines

guard

engine

buffers

buffet car

carriages

engine driver

goods train

platform

signals

ticket collector

suitcases

headlights

oil can

engine

battery

petrol lorry

AIR

The airport

air hostess

helicopter

runway

aeroplane

control tower

pilot

car wash

boot

air pump

petrol pump

wheel spanner tyre bonnet breakdown lorry oil

CAR WASH CAR WASH

21

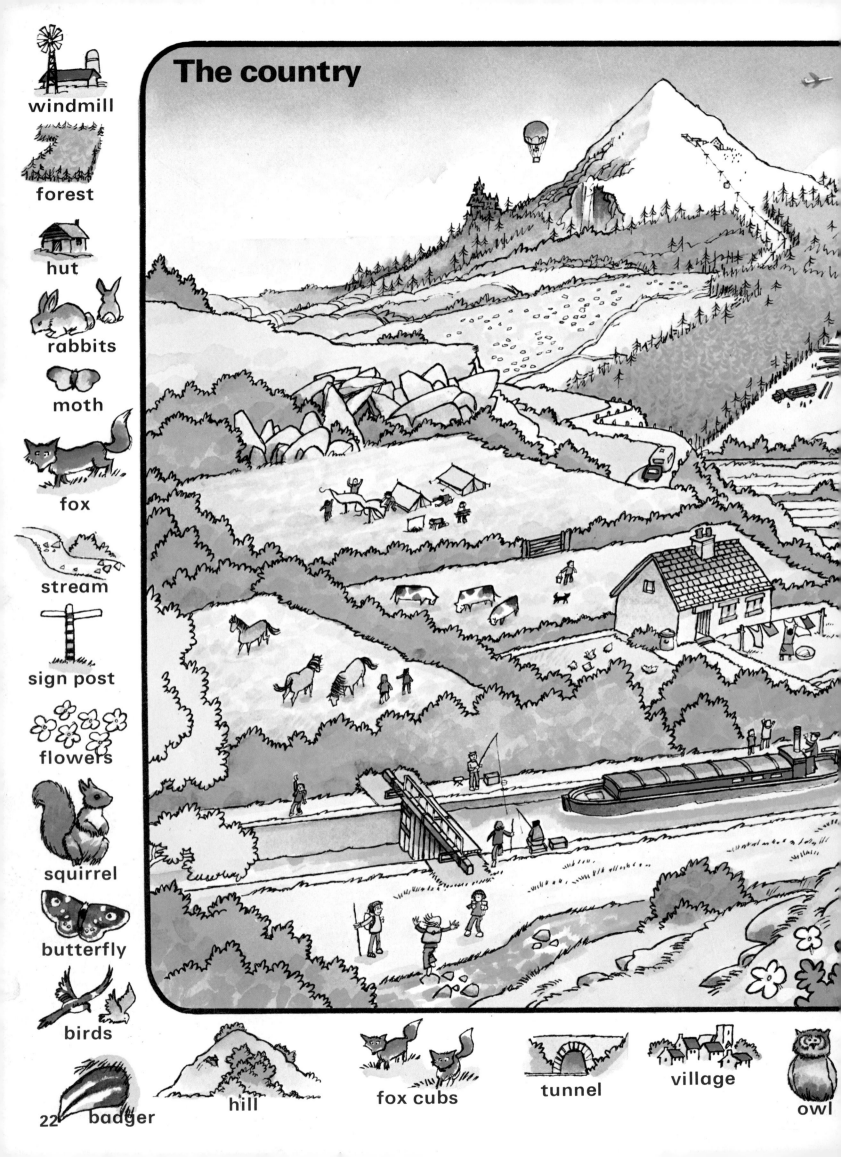

The country

windmill

forest

hut

rabbits

moth

fox

stream

sign post

flowers

squirrel

butterfly

birds

badger

hill

fox cubs

tunnel

village

owl

22

balloon

caravan

logs

tents

road

bridge

barge

waterfall

mountain

stones

mole

train

river

canal

rocks

fisherman

lock

23

The farm

pond

sheep

haystack

ducks

trailer

lambs

fence

loft

pigsty

bull

mud

piglets

barn

stable

24 cart

farmer

pony

tractor

saddle

geese

straw bales

sacks

lorry

orchard

hen house

cowshed

cow

ducklings

cock

calf

plough

shepherd

sheep dog

turkeys

scarecrow

hens

chicks

pigs

horse

goslings

field

hay

corn

farmhouse

25

The seaside

sailing boat

sea

oar

lighthouse

spade

bucket

star fish

sandcastle

gull

flag

crab

sailor

sun hat

buoy   island   harbour   deck chair   motor boat   water skier

26

waves

seashell

cliff

ship

canoe

pebbles

ball

rocks

flippers

sea weed

net

paddle

fishing boat

umbrella

donkey

oil tanker

rowing boat

swimsuit

rope

At school

aquarium

badge

ceiling

pencils

boys

calendar

wall

wastepaper bin

scissors

4+2 =
3 -2 =

sums

ruler

desk

photographs

paints

paper

brushes

bell

a b c d e f g
h i j k l m n o
p q r s t u v
w x y z

alphabet

boxes

books

abcdefg
hijklmno
pqrstuv
wxyz

painting

pens

chalk

easel

floor

plants

girls

globe

glue

door handle

note book

drawing pins

drawing

map

crayons

lamp

blackboard

blind

rubber

teacher

29

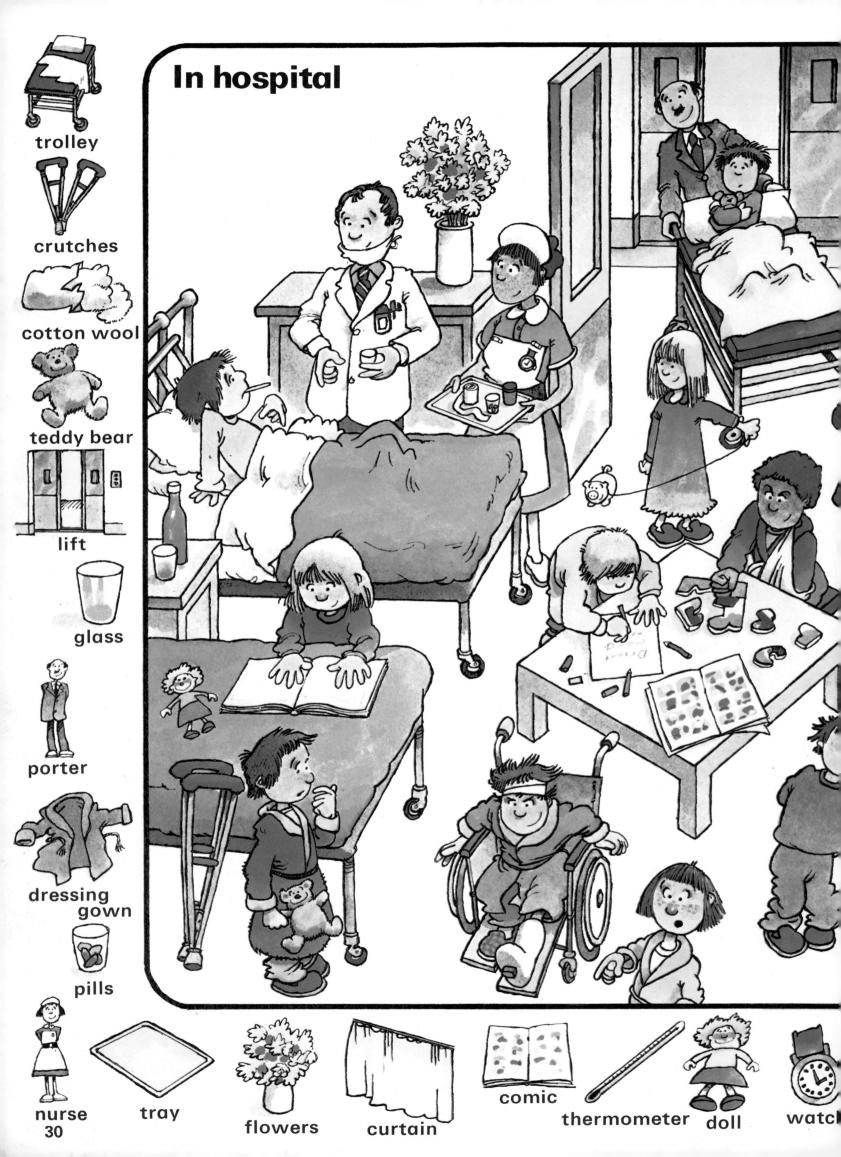

In hospital

trolley

crutches

cotton wool

teddy bear

lift

glass

porter

dressing gown

pills

nurse

30

tray

flowers

curtain

comic

thermometer

doll

watch

locker

medicine

slippers

pyjamas

syringe

squash

nightdress

cupboard

television

bed

chart

plaster

bandage

black eye

wheelchair

jigsaw

doctor 31

The party

balloons

sparklers

paper hats

trifle

sandwiches

moon

sweets

biscuits

table cloth

records

cake

chocolate

buns

lantern

toys

ribbon

candles

straws

stars

parcels

pudding

presents

window

jelly

fireworks

paper chains

costume 33

The shop

bananas

grapefruit

lettuce

grapes

cauliflower

apples

carrots

leek

pumpkin

cucumber

lemons

celery

beans

cherries

apricots

cabbage

melon

CHEESE

MEAT

FRUIT

FRUIT

VEGETABLES

mushrooms

tomatoes

peas

plums

raspberries

onions

peaches

pineapple

potatoes

spinach

34

FISH

BREAD

GROCERIES

tins

bread

butter

cheese

chicken

eggs

fish

flour

jars

meat

sausages

yoghurt

basket

bottles

prouts

oranges

strawberries

bags

cash desk

scales

money

purse

trolley

handbag

35

Food

breakfast

lunch or dinner

coffee

chicken

jam

fried eggs

milk

honey

hot chocolate

chops

cream

beer

ham

salt

pepper

supper or dinner

tea

fruit juice

nuts

meat

sugar

soup

omelette

salad

stew

pancakes

rolls

rice

wine

spaghetti

sauce

37

Me

hair   eyebrow   eye   nose   cheek

mouth   lips   teeth   tongue   chin

neck   ears   head   face   shoulders

arms   elbow   hands   fingers   thumbs

back   bottom   chest   tummy   knees

legs   feet   toes   heel

My clothes

pants

vest

trousers

jeans

t-shirt

skirt

shirt

tie

shorts

socks

sweater

jumper

cardigan

tights

blouse

dress

gymshoes

shoes

sandals

boots

gloves

jacket

anorak

coat

handkerchief

cap

hat

belt

buttons

button holes

pockets

zip

buckle

laces

scarf

People

actor

chef

dancer

carpenter

frogman

astronaut

conductor

clown

soldier

policeman

farmer

singer

shop-keeper

racing-car driver

mechanic

artist

butcher

fireman

postman

deep-sea diver

painter

train driver

mountaineer

judge

dentist

zoo-keeper

pilot

baker

Families

father
husband

mother
wife

daughter
sister

son
brother

aunt

uncle

cousin

grandmother

grandfather

Doing things

smile

carry

bath

think

write

crawl

build

paint

chop

read

clean

listen

cut

break

fall

wash

hide

drink

sweep

wash

laugh

cry

dance

catch

knit

sit

blow

climb

play

cook

fight

sleep

wait

skip

pick

watch

throw

talk

pull

take

eat

sew

sing

win

run

jump

dig

make

buy

walk

push

stand

Opposite words

good

bad

small

big

fat

thin

half

whole

cold

hot

top

bottom

soft

hard

first

last

far

few

many

near

high

low

empty

full

dirty

clean

left

44

slow

fast

easy

difficult

long

short

nice

nasty

upstairs

downstairs

over

under

front

back

wet

dry

alive

dead

dark

light

open   closed

right

old

new

out

in

45

Storybook words

giant

castle

dragon   knight

broomstick   witch

pistol

cannon   pirate   treasure

wand

toadstool   elf

dwarf

fairy   wishing well

magician

robber   desert   Indian   sheriff   cowboy   stage coach

devil

crown

pageboy

princess

prince

sword

queen

king

palace

angel

dinosaur

prison

reindeer

sleigh

Father Christmas

wizard

ghost

bridegroom

bride

bridesmaids

monster

Pets

rabbits

cat

dog

goldfish

lizards

parrot

frogs

budgerigars

hedgehog

silk worms

hamster

toads

puppies

pigeons

snakes

kittens

mice

tortoises

Weather

clouds

fog

rain

frost

snow

sun

rainbow

lightning

dew

wind

mist

Seasons

spring

summer

autumn

winter

Sports

boxing

cycle racing

baseball

swimming

football

gymnastics

high jump

skiing

motor racing

tennis

horse racing

skating

shooting

cricket

weight-lifting

show jumping

speedway racing

riding

sailing

table tennis

rowing

wrestling

basket ball

judo

Colours

black

orange

green

red

pink

blue

white

brown

grey

purple

yellow

Shapes

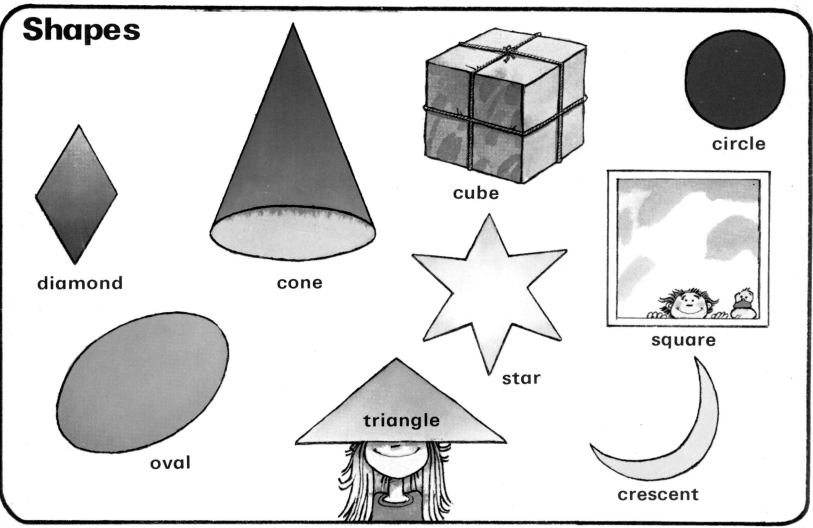

diamond

cone

cube

circle

oval

triangle

star

square

crescent

Numbers

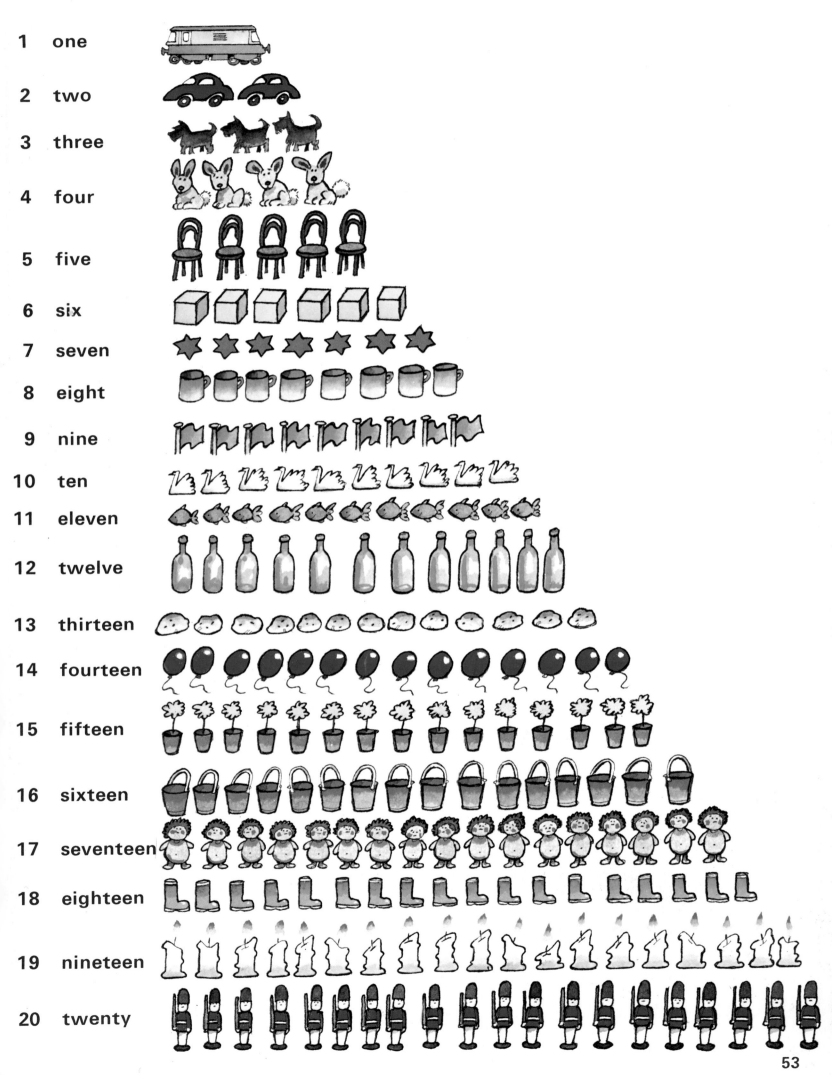

1	one
2	two
3	three
4	four
5	five
6	six
7	seven
8	eight
9	nine
10	ten
11	eleven
12	twelve
13	thirteen
14	fourteen
15	fifteen
16	sixteen
17	seventeen
18	eighteen
19	nineteen
20	twenty

The fairground

roundabout

mat

helter skelter

big wheel

dodgems

big dipper

hoop-la

pop corn

candy floss

ghost train

rifle range

The circus

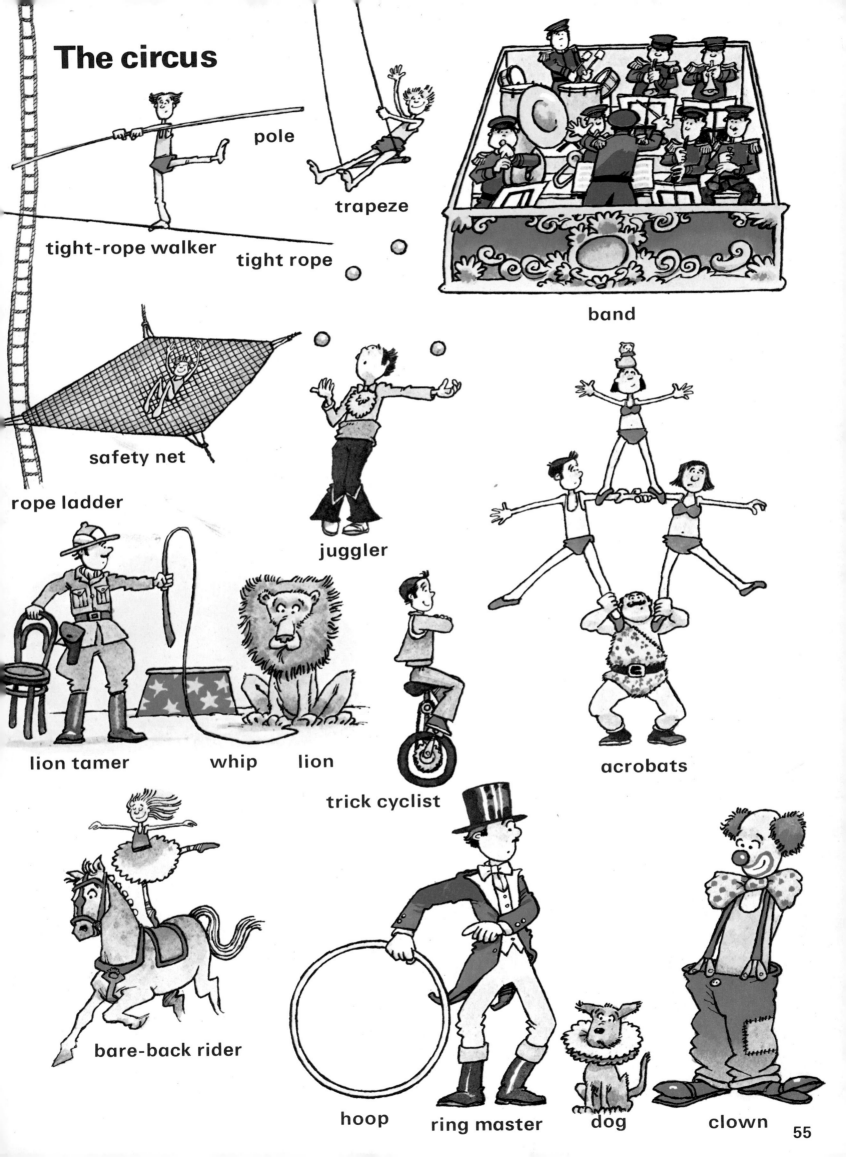

pole

trapeze

tight-rope walker

tight rope

band

safety net

rope ladder

juggler

acrobats

lion tamer   whip   lion

trick cyclist

bare-back rider

hoop   ring master   dog   clown

Words without pictures

Lots of words to read, say and spell

about
across
after
afternoon
again
along
all
always
am
and
another
are
as
ask
at
away

be
beautiful
because
before
behind
birthday
bought
bring
brought
burn
busy
but
by

call
came
can
chase
come
corner
could
crash

day
die
do

each
early
end
evening
every

feed
feel
fetch
find
finish
for
friend
from

game
get
give
glad
go
gone
ground
grow

happy
has
have
had
hear
heavy
help
her
here
him
his
hold
hungry
hurt

I
if
ill
is
it

jungle
just

keep
knock
know

late
leave
learn
less
let
like
line
look
lot
love
lovely

magic
meet
mend
might
month
morning
move
my
myself

name
never
next
night
no
now

of
off
once
other
our
own

pattern
please
poor
pretty
put

rich
round

sad
say
see
sell
shall
she
shine
should
show
sick
so
soon
some
sorry
speak
start
stay
stop

tell
thank
that
the
their
them
then
there
these
they
thing
thirsty
this
time
tired
to

today
tonight
tomorrow
too
try

ugly
us
use
useful

very

want
was
way
we
week
went
were
what
when
where
which
while
who
whose
why
with
work
would

year
yes
yesterday
you

Sunday
Monday
Tuesday
Wednesday
Thursday
Friday
Saturday

January
February
March
April
May
June
July
August
September
October
November
December

Words in order

This is a list of all the words in the pictures. They are in the same order as the alphabet. After each word is a number. This is the page number. On that page you will find the word and a picture.

a

acrobats, 55
actor, 40
aerial, 13
air hostess, 21
airport, 21
air pump, 21
alive, 45
alphabet, 28
ambulance, 12
animals, 18 and 19
angel, 47
anorak, 38
ant, 8
ape, 19
apple, 34
apricot, 34
apron, 6
aquarium, 28
arrow, 15
arm, 38
artist, 40
astronaut, 40
aunt, 41
autumn, 49
axe, 11

b

baby, 17
back, 45
back (of body), 38
bad, 44
badge, 28
badger, 24
bag, 35
baker, 4

ball, 16, 27
balloon, 23, 32
banana, 34
band, 55
bandage, 31
bare-back rider, 55
barge, 23
barn, 24
barrel, 11
baseball, 50
basket, 35
basketball, 51
bat (animal), 18
bat (for hitting), 14
bath, 4
bath, have a, 42
bathroom, 4
battery, 20
beads, 14
beans, 34
bear, 18
bear, polar, 19
beaver, 18
bed, 5, 31
bedroom, 5
bee, 9
beehive, 8
beer, 36
bell, 28
belt, 39
bench (park), 17
bench (work), 11
bicycle, 12
big, 44
big dipper, 54
big wheel, 54
birds, 17, 22
birds' nest, 9
biscuit, 32
black, 52
blackboard, 28
black eye, 31
blind (window), 29
blouse, 39
blow, 43
blue, 52
boat, 15
body words, 38
bolt, 9
bone, 8
bonfire, 9
bonnet (of car), 21
book, 28
bookcase, 4
boot (for foot), 39
boot (of car), 21
bottle, 35
bottom (of body), 38

bottom (drawer), 44
bow, 15
bowl, 7
boxes, 28
boxing, 50
boy, 28
bread, 35
break, 42
breakdown lorry, 21
breakfast, 36
bricks, 8
bride, 47
bridegroom, 47
bridesmaids, 47
bridge, 23
broom, 7, 9
broomstick, 46
brother, 41
brown, 52
brush, 5, 7, 28
bubbles, 4
bucket, 26
buckle, 39
budgerigars, 48
buffalo, 19
buffers (train), 20
buffet car, 20
build, 42
bulb (light), 7
bull, 24
bun, 32
buoy, 26
bus, 13
bush, 16
butcher, 41
butter, 35
butterfly, 22
button, 39
button hole, 39
buy, 43

c

cabbage, 34
café, 12
cake, 32
calendar, 28
calf, 25
camel, 19
camera, 14
canal, 23

candle, 33
candy floss, 54
cannon, 14, 46
canoe, 27
cap, 39
car, 13
car wash, 21
caravan, 23
cards, 14
cardigan, 39
carpenter, 40
carpet, 4
carriage, 20
carrot, 34
carry, 42
cart, 24
cash desk, 35
castle, 15, 46
cat, 48
catch, 42
caterpillar, 8
cauliflower, 34
ceiling, 27
celery, 34
chair, 4
chalk, 29
chart, 31
cheek, 38
cheese, 34, 35
chef, 40
cherry, 34
chest (body), 38
chest-of-drawers, 5
chick, 25
chicken, 35, 36
children, 16
chimney, 12
chin, 38
chocolate, 32
chop (wood), 42
chops (meat), 36
church, 13
cinema, 13
circle, 52
circus, 54 and 55
clay, 15
clean, 44
clean (to), 42
cliff, 27
climb, 43
clock, 4, 6
closed, 45
clothes, 5, 39
clouds, 49
clown, 40, 55
coat, 39
cobweb, 3
cock, 25
coffee, 36
cold, 44
colours, 52
comb, 5

comic, 30
conductor, 40
cone, 52
control tower, 21
cook, 43
cooker, 7
corn, 25
costume, 33
cotton wool, 30
country, 22 and 23
cousin, 41
cow, 25
cowboy, 46
cowshed, 25
crab, 26
crane, 14
crawl, 42
crayon, 29
cream, 36
crescent, 52
cricket (sport), 51
crocodile, 18
crossing (road), 12
crown, 46
crutches, 30
cry, 42
cub, fox, 22
cub, lion, 18
cube, 52
cucumber, 34
cup, 7
cupboard, 7, 31
cushion, 4
curtain, 30
cut, 42
cycle racing, 50

d

dance, 42
dancer, 40
dark, 45
daughter, 41
dead, 45
deck chair, 26
deep-sea diver, 40
deer, 19
demon, 47
dentist, 41
desert, 46
desk, 28
dew, 49
diamond, 52
dice, 14

difficult, 45
digger, 13
dig, 43
dinner, 36, 37
dinosaur, 47
dirty, 44
diver, 41
doctor, 31
dodgems, 54
dog, 16, 48, 55
dog lead, 17
doing words, 42 and 43
doll, 14, 30
dolls' house, 14
dolphin, 19
donkey, 27
door, 6
door handle, 28
downstairs, 45
dragon, 46
drawer, 7
drawing, 29
drawing pin, 29
dress, 39
dressing gown, 30
drill (road), 12
drill (wood), 10
drink, 42
driver, 13
drum, 15
dry, 45
duck, 17, 24
ducklings, 17
dustbin, 8
duster, 6
dustpan, 7
dwarf, 46

e

eagle, 18
ear, 38
earth, 17
easel, 29
easy, 45
eat, 43
egg, 35
egg (fried), 36
eiderdown, 5
eight, 53
eighteen, 53
elbow, 38
elephant, 19

eleven, 53
elf, 46
engine (car), 20
engine (railway), 20
engine driver, 20
empty, 44
eye, 38
eyebrow, 38

f

face, 38
factory, 13
fairground, 54
fairy, 46
fall, 42
family, 41
far, 44
farm, 24 and 25
farmer, 24, 40
farmhouse, 25
fast, 45
fat, 44
father, 41
Father Christmas, 47
feathers, 18
feet, 38
fence, 24
few, 44
field, 25
fifteen, 53
fight, 42
file, 10
finger, 38
fire, 9
fire engine, 13
fireman, 41
firewood, 10
firework, 33
first, 44
fish, 35
fisherman, 23
fishing boat, 27
fishing rod, 15
five, 53
flag, 26
flats, 12
flippers, 27
floor, 29
flour, 35
flower, 8, 17, 22, 30
flowerbed, 17
fly, 5
fog, 49

food, 36 and 37
foot, 38
football, 50
forest, 22
fork (garden), 9
fork (table), 6
four, 53
fourteen, 53
fox, 22
fox cubs, 22
fried eggs, 36
frog, 16, 48
frogman, 40
front, 45
frost, 49
fruit, 34
fruit juice, 37
frying pan, 7
full, 44

g

garage, 12, 20 and 21
garden, 8 and 9
gate, 16
geese, 24
ghost, 47
ghost train, 54
giant, 46
giraffe, 18
girl, 29
glass (drinking), 6, 30
globe, 29
gloves, 39
glue, 29
goat, 19
goldfish, 48
good, 44
goods train, 20
goose, 24
gorilla, 18
gosling, 25
grandfather, 41
grandmother, 41
grape, 33
grapefruit, 34
grass, 9
green, 52
greenhouse, 9
grey, 52
groceries, 35
guard (railway), 20
guitar, 14

gull, 26
gun, 15
gutter, 8
gymnastics, 50
gymshoes, 39

h

hair, 38
half, 44
hall, 5
ham, 36
hammer, 10
hamster, 48
hand, 38
handbag, 35
handkerchief, 39
handle (door), 29
harbour, 26
hard, 44
hat, 39
hay, 25
haystack, 24
head, 38
headlights, 20
hedge, 8
hedgehog, 48
heel, 38
helicopter, 21
helter skelter, 54
hen, 25
hen house, 25
hide, 42
high, 44
high jump, 50
hill, 22
hippopotamus, 18
hoe, 9
hole, 12
hoop, 55
hoop-la, 54
home, 4 and 5
horns, 19
horse, 25
horse racing, 50
horse rider, 51
hose pipe, 9
hospital, 30 and 31
hot, 44
hot chocolate, 36
hotel, 12
house, 13
husband, 41
hut, 22

i

ice cream, 16
in, 45
Indian, 46
iron, 6
ironing board, 7
island, 26

j

jacket, 39
jam, 36
jars, 10, 35
jeans, 39
jelly, 33
jigsaw, 31
judge, 41
judo, 51
juggler, 55
jump, 43
jumper, 39

k

kangaroo, 18
kettle, 6
key, 7
king, 47
kitchen, 6 and 7
kite, 16
kittens, 48
knee, 38
knife, 6
knight, 46
knit, 42

l

laces (shoe), 39
ladder, 11
lake, 17
lamb, 24
lamp, 4, 29
lamp post, 13
lantern, 32
last, 44
laugh, 42
lawn mower, 9
leaf, 9
leaves, 9
leeks, 34
left, 44
leg, 38
lemons, 34
leopard, 19
letter, 5
lettuce, 34
lift, 30
light, 45
lighthouse, 26
lightning, 49
lion, 18, 55
lion tamer, 55
lips, 38
listen, 42
living room, 4
lizards, 48
lock (canal), 23
locker, 31
loft, 24
logs, 23
long, 45
lorry, 12, 25
low, 44
lunch, 36

m

magician, 46
make, 43
man, 12
many, 44

map, 29
marbles, 14
market, 13
mask, 15
mat, 54
matches, 7
meals, 36, 37
meat, 35, 37
mechanic, 40
medicine, 31
melon, 34
milk, 36
mirror, 5
mist, 49
mole, 23
money, 35
money box, 15
monkey, 18
monster, 47
moon, 32
mop, 6
moth, 22
mother, 41
motor boat, 26
motor cycle, 13
motor racing, 50
mountain, 23
mountaineer, 41
mouth, 38
mouth organ, 14
mud, 24
mushroom, 34

n

nails, 11
nasty, 45
near, 44
neck, 38
nest, birds', 9
net, 27
new, 45
newspaper, 5
nice, 45
nightdress, 31
nine, 53
nineteen, 53
nose, 38
notebook, 29
numbers, 53
nurse, 30
nuts (for bolts), 11
nuts (to eat), 37

o

p

q

r

roll (bread), 37
roller, 12, 14
roller skates, 16
roof, 13
rope, 27
rope ladder, 55
roundabout, 54
rowing, 51
rowing boat, 27
rubber, 28
rubbish, 7
rug, 4
ruler, 28
run, 43
runway, 21

S

sacks, 24
saddle, 24
safety net, 54
sailing, 51
sailing boat, 26
sailor, 26
salad, 37
salt, 36
sandals, 39
sandcastle, 26
sandpaper, 10
sandpit, 16
sandwich, 32
sauce, 37
saucepan, 6
saucer, 6
sausages, 35
saw, 10
sawdust, 10
scales, 35
scarecrow, 25
school, 12, 28 and 29
scissors, 28
scooter, 16
screw, 11
screwdriver, 10
sea, 26
sea shell, 27
seal, 19
seaside, 26 and 27
seasons, 49
seaweed, 27
seeds, 8
seesaw, 17
seven, 53
seventeen, 53
sew, 43

shapes, 52
shark, 19
shavings, 10
shed, 8
sheep, 24
sheepdog, 25
sheet, 5
shepherd, 25
sheriff, 46
ship, 27
shirt, 39
shoe, 39
shooting, 51
shop, 12, 34 and 35
shopkeeper, 40
short, 45
shorts, 39
shoulder, 38
show jumping, 51
shower, 4
signals, 20
signpost, 22
silkworms, 48
sing, 43
singer, 40
sink, 6
sister, 41
sit, 42
six, 53
sixteen, 53
scarf, 39
skating, 50
skiing, 50
skip, 43
skipping rope, 17
skirt, 39
sleep, 43
sleigh, 47
slide, 16
slippers, 31
slow, 45
small, 44
smile, 42
smoke, 9
snail, 8
snake, 48
snow, 49
soap, 4
socks, 39
soft, 44
soldier, 40
soldiers (toy), 15
son, 41
soup, 37
spaceman, 14
spade, 8, 26
spaghetti, 37
spanner, 21
sparklers, 32
speedway racing, 51
spider, 5
spinach, 34

sponge, 4
spoon, 6
sports, 50 and 51
sprinkler, 8
spring, 49
sprouts, 35
square, 52
squash, 31
squirrel, 22
stable, 24
stagecoach, 46
stairs, 5
station, 20
stand, 43
star, 33, 52
star fish, 26
statue, 13
steps, 12
stew, 37
sticks, 9
stones, 23
stool, 6
storybook words, 46 and 47
straw (drinking), 33
straw bale, 24
strawberry, 35
stream, 22
street, 12 and 13
string, 16
submarine, 15
sugar, 37
suitcases, 20
summer, 49
sums, 28
sun, 49
sun hat, 26
supper, 37
swan, 17
sweater, 39
sweep, 42
sweets, 32
swimming, 50
swimsuit, 27
swings, 16
switch, 6
sword, 47
syringe, 31

t

table, 4, 7
table cloth, 32
table tennis, 51
tacks, 10